Roc...

CROOK CATCHERS

The Minestrone Mob

Karen Wallace &
Judy Brown

A & C Black • London

Rockets

CROOK CATCHERS

Karen Wallace & Judy Brown

The Stuff-it-in Specials
The Minestrone Mob
The Sandwich Scam
The Peanut Prankster

First paperback edition 2000
First published 1999 in hardback by
A & C Black (Publishers) Ltd
35 Bedford Row, London WC1R 4JH

Text copyright © 1999 Karen Wallace
Illustrations copyright © 1999 Judy Brown

The right of Karen Wallace and Judy Brown to be
identified as author and illustrator of this work has
been asserted by them in accordance with the
Copyright, Designs and Patents Act 1988.

ISBN 0-7136-5126-1

A CIP catalogue record for this book is available
from the British Library.

All rights reserved. No part of this publication may
be reproduced in any form or by any means - graphic,
electronic or mechanical, including photocopying,
recording, taping or information storage and retrieval
systems - without the prior permission in writing of
the publishers.

Printed and bound by G. Z. Printek, Bilbao, Spain.

Chapter One

Lettuce Leef and Nimble Charlie were Crook Catchers to the Queen.

Their pumpkin office was connected to the Palace by a special emergency telephone.

Now it was ringing!

'Sounds like an emergency to me!'
Nimble Charlie muttered.
Lettuce Leef headed for the door.

The Palace door opened before the
Crook Catchers even had time to knock.
Lettuce Leef gasped.

Splatter, the Queen's trusty servant, was
standing in his underwear!

'What happened to your uniform?' asked Nimble Charlie trying not to stare.

Lettuce Leef hid a smile. Splatter's vest was embroidered with bunny rabbits.

'Splatter!' bellowed the Queen from
inside the Palace.

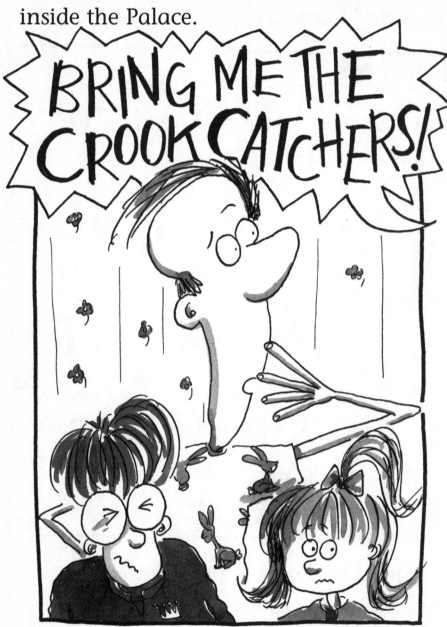

Chapter Two

The Queen's room was in a terrible mess!
Cookery books and bits of paper covered
the floor.

Most extraordinary of all, the Queen was
standing in the middle of the room in
her underwear!

Lettuce Leef bowed
so she didn't have
to look.

Nimble Charlie
curtseyed
by mistake.

Splatter quickly held out the Queen's
dressing gown.

'Your Majesty,' said Nimble Charlie gently. 'What's going on?'

'Who's Prince Linguini?' asked Lettuce Leef. 'And why aren't you wearing any clothes?'

'They were stolen,' muttered Splatter.
The Queen held up a copy of
the *Daily Screamer*.

ONE SLURP AND YOU'RE HOOPED!
PRINCE LINGUINI ARRIVES IN TOWN

Lettuce Leef and Nimble Charlie
exchanged looks. What was going on?

'The Queen and Prince Linguini are swapping royal gifts today,' explained Splatter. 'A truck load of his famous spaghetti hoops for fifty barrels of her home-made minestrone soup!'

Nimble Charlie thought hard.
The stolen clothes and the stolen recipe
had to be connected.

Splatter blushed and twirled a piece of hair in his fingers.

'What did they want?' asked
Nimble Charlie.
'They said they were tourists,'
mumbled Splatter.

They asked if they could look around.

'We hope you told them to get stuffed!'
bellowed the Queen.
Splatter swallowed hard.

The Queen took a step towards him.

Splatter opened his mouth but the only thing that came out was a small strangled squeak.

Chapter Three

The Queen's face was one inch from Splatter's nose.

Suddenly a tube of tomato paste whizzed through the open window.

It had a note tied to its neck.

The Queen stomped her foot and made a rude noise.

If these people think they can fool the Prince by dressing up in our clothes, they're out of their tiny minds!

Why's that?

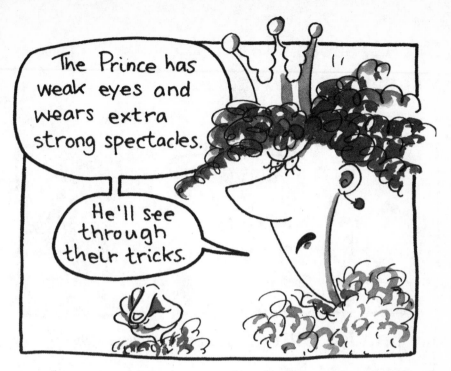

At that moment another tube of tomato paste whizzed through the window.

A pair of crushed spectacles was tied around its neck!

Nobody spoke.

Splatter began to shake.

'I forgot to tell you,' he whispered.

He handed Lettuce Leef a folded card.

She read it aloud.

**The Minestrone Mob
Wannabee Movie Moguls
but Mostly Thieves**

All payments in spaghetti hoops.
Prince Linguini's preferred.

The Queen stared at Splatter and went
black with rage.

Lettuce Leef and Nimble Charlie ran to
the door.

Chapter Four

Back in the pumpkin office, Lettuce Leef and Nimble Charlie looked at their clues.

'Where would you go if you were planning to trick a prince into thinking he was drinking soup with a queen?' muttered Lettuce Leef.

Nimble Charlie thought hard.

Lettuce Leef looked at the calling card.
'Wannabee Movie Moguls,' she muttered.

All afternoon Lettuce Leef and Nimble Charlie looked at movie sets.

But they didn't see one fake banqueting hall in one fake palace anywhere.

'Maybe I was wrong,' muttered Nimble Charlie as they turned down a fake tree-lined avenue. 'Maybe –'

'Maybe not!' Lettuce Leef pointed to a huge cardboard-looking castle at the end of the avenue. In front of it was an enormous truck.

Nimble Charlie peered through his extra-strong binoculars. A picture of a prince eating spaghetti hoops was painted on the side of the truck.

'Bullseye!' cried Nimble Charlie.

Lettuce Leef rang the Queen and made a plan.

Chapter Five

Inside the fake banqueting hall, Redbits was getting nervous. It was all very well dressing up as the Queen but it was another thing talking to Prince Linguini.

'Are we feeling quite well, Your Majesty?' murmured Prince Linguini. He felt his way around the banqueting table. Without his glasses, he couldn't see a thing.

Redbits jammed his tiara halfway down his head.

Prince Linguini pursed his lips. Perhaps the Queen had been watching too many cops and robbers movies. 'As you wish, Your Majesty,' he replied.

In front of Prince Linguini, the knives and forks and china were a blur. He found what he was looking for and tied his napkin around his neck.

In the kitchen of the cardboard palace, Sludge stirred a huge pot of the Queen's own minestrone.

He slurped a spoonful. It tasted really delicious. But nothing, absolutely nothing, was as delicious as Prince Linguini's spaghetti hoops.

His stomach rumbled and his hand trembled. Any minute now, a lifetime's supply would be theirs. He peeped into the banqueting hall.

Redbits and Prince Linguini were ready to do the deal.

Sludge climbed into Splatter's uniform and picked up the pot of soup.

Suddenly Nimble Charlie jumped out from his hiding place. He whipped a thick black sack over Sludge's head.

WHOOMPH!

A few seconds later, the real Splatter picked up the huge soup pot and headed for the banqueting hall.

Chapter Six

Underneath the banqueting table, Lettuce Leef explained her plan to the Queen.

Swap places when I give the signal.

But won't Prince Linguini see the difference between me and a fake Queen?

It was a tricky question. Apart from Redbits's voice and the stubble on his chin, there wasn't a lot to choose between them.

At that moment a marvellous, mouth-watering smell wafted through the air. It was the Queen's own minestrone!

'The soup awaits, Your Majesty,' murmured the real Splatter.

There was no time to lose!
Lettuce Leef and the Queen crawled up
to the end of the table.

Redbits's dirty trainers poked out from
under the Queen's best ball gown.

Softly and silently Lettuce Leef untied the
laces and tied them around the chair legs.

Above there was a clatter of spoons and bowls.

Soup is served.

Before Redbits had time to pick up his spoon -

WHOOMPH!

Nimble Charlie jumped from his hiding place and whipped a thick black sack over his head. Then he tipped back the chair and dragged Redbits away.

In the same moment, Lettuce Leef grabbed another chair. 'Go!' she whispered to the Queen.

Quick as a flash, the Queen threw herself into the new chair. Luckily Prince Linguini was so busy slurping his soup he didn't notice a thing!

That moment, Splatter dragged Redbits and Sludge into the room.

The Queen prodded Redbits in the stomach. 'If they can make one pot of my own Minestrone, they can make fifty barrels for Prince Linguini!'

She banged her fist on the table.

The Queen jumped on to the table.

The End